Time Loop Bunny Adventure

Written By Jason Koo & Rick Tinney
Illustrated By Rick Tinney

This book is dedicated to Reina, Reon, Renan, Ilayda and all the children who are brave enough to use their imaginations to open portals and jump in.

Look! Behind the bush. **SHHHHH...**
Bunny ears are sticking out. Let's sneak up to it.

The bunny is floating quietly. It is sleeping.
What does the note say?

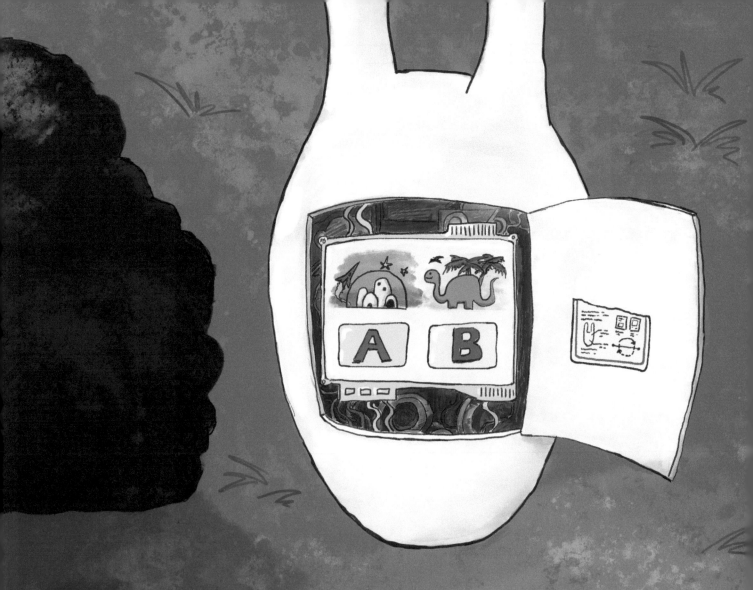

A panel is open on the bunny's back. Inside there is a screen with two buttons. Which one looks like more fun?
Press A or B.

A speaker inside the bunny squeaks with a loud robot voice...

"Activating Temporal Whirlpool — Please stand back."

Go to page 7.

The bunny wakes up and starts flying in circles, creating a swirly portal.
The portal spins around fast, making it very windy. *WOOOOOSHHHHH!*
We are getting sucked in! *WOOOOOSHHHHHH SSSSLLLLUUURP!!!*
If you pressed button A go to page 8, for button B go to page 18.

SHHHPLLLOOOOOOP!
The bunny's portal spits out into a city on another planet. All of the buildings are inside huge bubbles. What are the bubbles for?

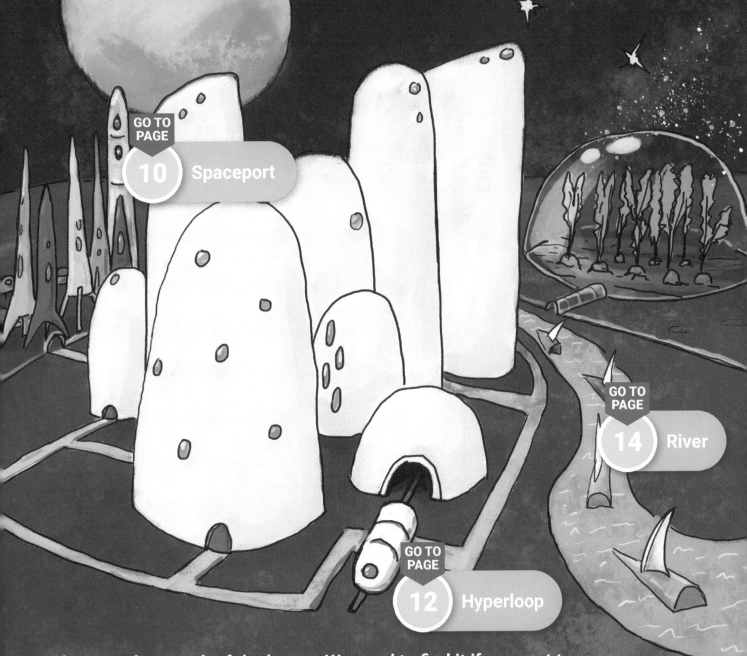

GO TO PAGE

10 Spaceport

GO TO PAGE

14 River

GO TO PAGE

12 Hyperloop

Oh no, we lost track of the bunny. We need to find it if we want to get back home. Where should we look?

Go to page 10 to look in the spaceport, or page 12 to check the hyperloop, or page 14 to explore the river.

There it is! The bunny is flying. It is weaving in between the rockets and spaceships. Are aliens parked here, too?

The bunny is SO fast! Let's chase it with one of these spaceships.
Pick a spaceship that looks fast then fly over to page 16.

The bunny is going into that hyperloop tunnel.
Quickly... get into this hyperloop pod to chase it.
No wait... it doesn't have wheels! How does it move?

The bunny is almost to the other stop! No time to waste.
How do we make this pod go? Press all the buttons!

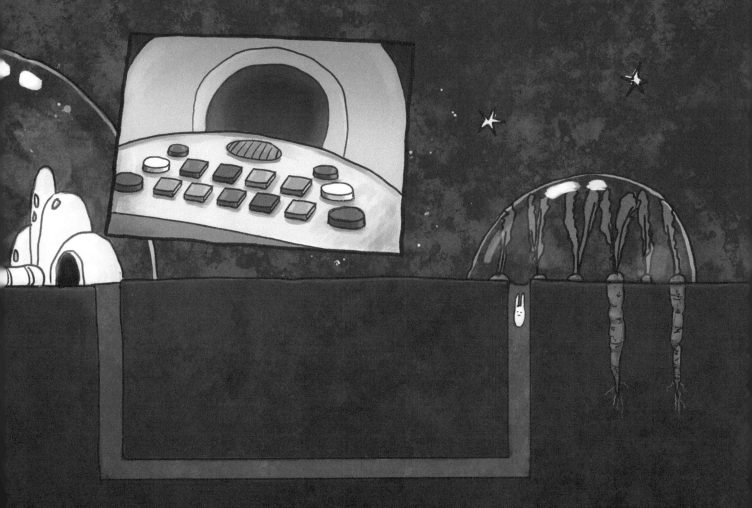

The pod starts and zips through the tunnel.
Catch up to the bunny on page 16.

13

The bunny is hopping across the river.
It is very wide. Can we swim across?

14

Let's be safe and take a boat instead.
The boats on this river look like
rocket ship nose cones. How interesting!
Pick the boat with the color you like then sail to page 16.

We chased the bunny to a farm.
Wow! The carrots here are humongous!
How do they grow so big?

Whatever is in those barrels looks disgusting.
I wonder where the bunny is hiding?
Catch the bunny on page 28.

GO TO PAGE
24 Cave

GO TO PAGE
22 River

SHHHPLLLOOOOOOP!

The bunny's portal has dropped us into a thick jungle. Look! Dinosaurs are swimming in that river. Others are flying high, circling their nests. A big cave opens on the side of the mountain.

GO TO PAGE

20 Mountain

The bunny floats away, following a jungle trail.
If we run ahead, maybe we can catch it coming out.
Climb to page 20 to snatch it on top of the mountain, or swim to page 22
to catch the bunny by the river, or take a peek into the cave on page 24.

Oh my! The bunny is flying around with these pterodactyls. The bunny has no wings. How in the world does it fly? We'll never catch it so high in the sky.

Oh good! It's landing behind this mountain peak.

Climb after the bunny to page 26.

The bunny is already on the other side of the river. It has no fins like those plesiosaurs. How did it get across so quickly?

One friendly dinosaur gives us a ride across the river. But hurry! The bunny is already headed up the mountain.
Hurry up to page 26.

Inside the cave, many small oryctodromeus are playing hide-and-seek with their babies. The bunny is floating deeper and deeper into the cave.

It is so dark in this tunnel. We need a flashlight. *SHHHHH...*
Do you hear that? Is that the bunny whistling?
Follow with your ears to page 26.

What is the bunny doing? Is it going to eat those eggs? Oh no!

Well, how clever! The bunny blends in with the eggs in this nest.
Let's see, where is it? Grab the bunny on page 28.

The screen has three buttons now. The new button has a picture of a house. If we push that button, it might take us home. Which one should we push? Open a new portal by pressing A, B, or C. Go to page 8 if you press A, or page 18 if you press B, or page 30 if you press C.

PLUNK!
This portal opens at home. Everything in the room
is blowing around, but slowly drops to the floor as
the portal shrinks and disappears into the wall.
SHHHWAMM-PU!!!

The bunny hides behind the bush again. Its ears are sticking out. Its tiny robot eyes are closing as it falls asleep. I wonder if it will still be there tomorrow? We'll find out. Good night!

CPSIA information can be obtained
at www.ICGtesting.com
Printed in the USA
LVHW071208260422
717236LV00024B/1190